ANNE FINE

The Diary of a
Killer Cat

Illustrated by Steve Cox

PUFFIN

PUFFIN BOOKS

Published by the Penguin Group
Penguin Books Ltd, 80 Strand, London WC2R ORL, England
Penguin Group (USA), Inc., 375 Hudson Street, New York, New York 10014, USA
Penguin Books Australia Ltd, 250 Camberwell Road, Camberwell, Victoria 3124, Australia
Penguin Books Canada Ltd, 10 Alcorn Avenue, Toronto, Ontario, Canada M4V 3B2
Penguin Books India (P) Ltd, 11 Community Centre, Panchsheel Park, New Delhi – 110 017, India
Penguin Books (NZ) Ltd, Cnr Rosedale and Airborne Roads, Albany, Auckland, New Zealand
Penguin Books (South Africa) (Pty) Ltd, 24 Sturdee Avenue, Rosebank 2196, South Africa

Penguin Books Ltd, Registered Offices: 80 Strand, London WC2R ORL, England

www.penguin.com

First published by Hamish Hamilton Ltd 1994
Published in Puffin Books 1996
This edition has been exclusively produced for Nestlé Cheerios and Honey Nut Cheerios 2004

1

Text copyright © Anne Fine, 1994
Illustrations copyright © Steve Cox, 1994
All rights reserved

The moral right of the author and illustrator has been asserted

Set in Baskerville

Made and printed in England by Clays Ltd, St Ives plc

British Library Cataloguing in Publication Data
A CIP catalogue record for this book is available from the British Library

ISBN 0-141-31829-5

1 : Monday

OKAY, OKAY. So hang me. I killed the bird. For pity's sake, I'm a *cat*. It's practically my *job* to go creeping round the garden after sweet little eensy-weensy birdy-pies that can hardly fly from one hedge to another. So what am I supposed to do when one of the poor feathery little flutterballs just about throws itself into my mouth? I mean, it practically landed on my paws. It could have *hurt* me.

Okay, *okay*. So I biffed it. Is that any reason for Ellie to cry in my fur so hard I almost *drown*, and squeeze me so hard I almost *choke*?

"Oh, Tuffy!" she says, all sniffles and red eyes and piles of wet tissues. "Oh, Tuffy. How could you *do* that?"

How could I *do* that? I'm a *cat*. How did I know there was going to be such a giant great fuss, with Ellie's mother rushing off to fetch sheets of old

newspaper, and Ellie's father filling a bucket with soapy water?

Okay, *okay*. So maybe I shouldn't have dragged it in and left it on the carpet. And maybe the stains won't come out, ever.

So *hang* me.

2: *Tuesday*

I QUITE ENJOYED the little funeral. I don't think they really wanted me to come, but, after all, it's just as much my garden as theirs. In fact, I spend a whole lot more time in it than they do. I'm the only one in the family who uses it properly.

Not that they're grateful. You ought to hear them.

"That cat is *ruining* my flower beds. There are hardly any of the petunias left."

"I'd barely *planted* the lobelias before it was lying on top of them, squashing

4

them flat."

"I *do* wish it wouldn't dig holes in the anemones."

Moan, moan, moan, moan. I don't know why they bother to keep a cat, since all they ever seem to do is complain.

5

All except Ellie. She was too busy being soppy about the bird. She put it in a box, and packed it round with cotton wool, and dug a little hole, and then we all stood round it while she said a few words, wishing the bird luck in heaven.

"Go away," Ellie's father hissed at me. (I find that man quite rude.) But I just flicked my tail at him. Gave him the blink. Who does he think he is? If I want to watch a little birdy's funeral, I'll watch it. After all, I've known the bird longer than any of them have. I knew it when it was *alive*.

3: Wednesday

SO SPANK ME! I brought a dead mouse into their precious house. I didn't even kill it. When I came across it, it was already a goner. Nobody's safe around here. This avenue is ankle-deep in rat poison, fast cars charge up and down at all hours, and I'm not the only cat around here. I don't even know what happened to the thing. All I know is, I found it. It was already dead. (Fresh dead, but dead.) And at the time I thought it was a good idea to bring it home. Don't ask me why. I must have been crazy. How did I know that Ellie

7

was going to grab me and give me one of her little talks?

"Oh, Tuffy! That's the second time this week. I can't bear it. I know you're a cat, and it's natural and everything. But please, for my sake, stop."

She gazed into my eyes.

"Will you stop? Please?"

I gave her the blink. (Well, I tried. But she wasn't having any.)

"I *mean* it, Tuffy," she told me. "I love you, and I understand how you feel. But you've got to stop doing this, okay?"

She had me by the paws. What could I say? So I tried to look all sorry. And then she burst into tears all over again, and we had another funeral.

This place is turning into Fun City. It really is.

8

4: Thursday

OKAY, OKAY! I'll try and explain about the rabbit. For starters, I don't think anyone's given me enough credit for getting it through the cat-flap. That was *not easy*. I can tell you, it took about an hour to get that rabbit through that little hole. That rabbit was downright *fat*. It was more like a pig than a rabbit, if you want my opinion.

Not that any of them cared what I thought. They were going mental.

"It's Thumper!" cried Ellie. "It's next-door's Thumper!"

"Oh, Lordy!" said Ellie's father. "Now we're in trouble. What are we going to do?"

Ellie's mother stared at me.

"How could a cat *do* that?" she asked. "I mean, it's not like a tiny bird, or a mouse, or anything. That rabbit is the same size as Tuffy. They both weigh a *ton*."

Nice. Very nice. This is my *family*, I'll have you know. Well, Ellie's family. But you take my point.

And Ellie, of course, freaked out. She went berserk.

"It's horrible," she cried. "*Horrible.* I can't believe that Tuffy could have done that. Thumper's been next door for years and years and years."

Sure. Thumper was a friend. I knew him well.

She turned on me.

"Tuffy! This is the end. That poor, poor rabbit. Look at him!"

And Thumper did look a bit of a mess, I admit it. I mean, most of it was only mud. And a few grass stains, I suppose. And there were quite a few bits of twig and stuff stuck in his fur. And he had a streak of oil on one ear. But no one gets dragged the whole way across a garden, and through a hedge, and over another garden, and through a freshly-oiled cat-flap, and ends up looking as if they're just off to a party.

And Thumper didn't care what he looked like. He was *dead*.

The rest of them minded, though. They minded a *lot*.

"What are we going to do?"

"Oh, this is dreadful. Next-door will never speak to us again."

"We must think of something."

And they did. I have to say, it was a brilliant plan, by any standards. First, Ellie's father fetched the bucket again, and filled it with warm soapy water. (He gave me a bit of a look as he did this, trying to make me feel guilty for the fact that he'd had to dip his hands in the old Fairy Liquid twice in one week. I just gave him my old 'I-am-not-impressed' stare back.)

Then Ellie's mother dunked Thumper in the bucket and gave him a nice bubbly wash and a swill-about. The water turned a pretty nasty brown colour. (All that mud.) And then, glaring at me as if it were all *my* fault, they tipped it down the sink and began over again with fresh soap suds.

Ellie was snivelling, of course.

"Do stop that, Ellie," her mother said. "It's getting on my nerves. If you

want to do something useful, go and
fetch the hairdrier.''

So Ellie trailed upstairs, still bawling
her eyes out.

I sat on the top of the dresser, and
watched them.

They up-ended poor Thumper and
dunked him again in the bucket.
(Good job he wasn't his old self. He'd
have hated all this washing.) And
when the water finally ran clear, they
pulled him out and drained him.

15

Then they plonked him on newspaper, and gave Ellie the hairdrier.

"There you go," they said. "Fluff him up nicely."

Well, she got right into it, I can tell you. That Ellie could grow up to be a real hot-shot hairdresser, the way she fluffed him up. I have to say, I never saw Thumper look so nice before, and he lived in next-door's hutch for years and years, and I saw him every day.

"Hiya, Thump," I'd sort of nod at him as I strolled over the lawn to check out what was left in the feeding bowls further down the avenue.

"IIi, Tuff," he'd sort of twitch back.

Yes, we were good mates. We were pals. And so it was really nice to see him looking so spruced up and smart when Ellie had finished with him.

He looked *good*.

"What now?" said Ellie's father.

Ellie's mum gave him a look – the sort of look she sometimes gives me, only nicer.

"Oh, no," he said. "Not me. Oh, no, no, no, no, no."

"It's you or me," she said. "And I can't go, can I?"

"Why not?" he said. "You're smaller than I am. You can crawl through the hedge easier."

That's when I realised what they had in mind. But what could I say? What could I do to stop them? To *explain*?

Nothing. I'm just a cat.

I sat and watched.

5: Friday

I CALL IT Friday because they left it so late. The clock was already well past midnight by the time Ellie's father finally heaved himself out of his comfy chair in front of the telly and went upstairs. When he came down again he was dressed in black. Black from head to foot.

"You look like a cat burglar," said Ellic's mother.

"I wish someone would burgle *our* cat," he muttered.

I just ignored him. I thought that was best.

19

Together they went to the back door.

"Don't switch the outside light on," he warned her. "You never know who might be watching."

I tried to sneak out at the same time,
but Ellie's mother held me back with
her foot.

"You can just stay inside tonight,"
she told me. "We've had enough
trouble from you this week."

Fair's fair. And I heard all about it anyway, later, from Bella and Tiger and Pusskins. They all reported back. (They're good mates.) They all saw Ellie's father creeping across the lawn, with his plastic bag full of Thumper (wrapped nicely in a towel to keep him clean). They all saw him forcing his way through the hole in the hedge, and crawling across next-door's lawn on his tummy.

"Couldn't think *what* he was doing," Pusskins said afterwards.

"*Ruined* the hole in the hedge," complained Bella. "He's made it so big that the Thompson's rottweiler could get through it now."

"That father of Ellie's must have the most dreadful night vision," said Tiger. "It took him forever to find that hutch in the dark."

"And prise the door open."

"And stuff in poor old Thumper."

"And set him out neatly on his bed of straw."

"All curled up."

"With the straw patted up round him."

"So it looked as if he was sleeping."

"It was very, very lifelike," said Bella. "It could have fooled me. If anyone just happened to be passing in the dark, they'd really have thought that poor old Thumper had just died happily and peacefully in his sleep, after a good life, from old age."

They all began howling with laughter.

"Sshh!" I said. "Keep it down, guys. They'll hear, and I'm not supposed to be out tonight. I'm grounded."

25

They all stared at me.

"Get away with you!"

"Grounded?"

"What *for*?"

"Murder," I said. "For cold-blooded bunnicide."

That set us all off again. We yowled and yowled. The last I heard before we took off in a gang up Beechcroft Drive was one of the bedroom windows being flung open, and Ellie's father yelling, "How did you get out, you crafty beast?"

So what's he going to do? Nail up the cat-flap?

6: *Still Friday*

HE NAILED UP the cat-flap. Would you *believe* this man? He comes down the stairs this morning, and before he's even out of his pyjamas he's set to work with the hammer and a nail.

Bang, bang, bang, bang!

I'm giving him the stare, I really am. But then he turns round and speaks to me directly.

"There," he says. "That'll fix you. Now it swings *this* way – " He gives the cat-flap a hefty shove with his foot. "But it doesn't swing *this* way."

And, sure enough, when the flap

tried to flap back in, it couldn't. It hit the nail.

"So," he says to me. "You can go out. Feel free to go out. Feel free, in fact, not only to go out, but also to stay out, get lost, or disappear for ever. But should you bother to come back again, don't go to the trouble of bringing anything with you. Because this is now a one-way flap, and so you will have to sit on the doormat until one of the family lets you in."

He narrows his eyes at me, all nasty-like.

"And woe betide you, Tuffy, if there's anything dead lying waiting on the doormat beside you."

'Woe betide you'! What a stupid expression. What on earth does it mean anyway? 'Woe betide you'!

Woe betide *him*.

7: *Saturday*

I HATE SATURDAY morning. It's so unsettling, all that fussing and door-banging and "Have you got the purse?" and "Where's the shopping list?" and "Do we need catfood?" Of course we need catfood. What else am I supposed to eat all week? Air?

They were all pretty quiet today, though. Ellie was sitting at the table carving Thumper a rather nice gravestone out of half a leftover cork floor tile. It said:

> Thumper
> Rest in peace

"You mustn't take it round next-door yet," her father warned her. "Not till they've told us Thumper's dead, at any rate."

Some people are born soft. Her eyes brimmed with tears.

"There goes Next-door now," Ellie's mother said, looking out of the window.

"Which way is she headed?"

"Towards the shops."

"Good. If we keep well behind, we can get Tuffy to the vet's without bumping into her."

Tuffy? Vet's?

Ellie was even more horrified than I was. She threw herself at her father, beating him with her soft little fists.

"Dad! No! You can't!"

I put up a far better fight with my claws. When he finally prised me out of the dark of the cupboard under the sink, his woolly was ruined and his hands were scratched and bleeding all over.

He wasn't very pleased about it.

"Come out of there, you great fat

furry psychopath. It's only a 'flu jab
you're booked in for – more's the
pity!''

Would *you* have believed him? I wasn't absolutely sure. (Neither was Ellie, so she tagged along.) I was still quite suspicious when we reached the vet's. That is *the only reason* why I spat at the girl behind the desk. There was no reason on earth to write HANDLE WITH CARE at the top of my case notes. Even the Thompson's rottweiler doesn't have HANDLE WITH CARE written on the top of his case notes. What's wrong with *me*?

So I was a little rude in the waiting room. So what? I *hate* waiting. And I especially hate waiting stuffed in a wire cat cage. It's cramped. It's hot. And it's boring. After a few hundred minutes of sitting there quietly, *anyone* would start teasing their neighbours. I didn't *mean* to frighten that little sick baby gerbil half to death. I was only *looking* at it. It's a free country, isn't it? Can't a cat even *look* at a sweet little baby gerbil?

And if I was licking my lips (which I wasn't) that's only because I was thirsty. Honestly. I wasn't trying to pretend I was going to eat it.

The trouble with baby gerbils is they can't take a *joke*.

And neither can anyone else round here.

Ellie's father looked up from the pamphlet he was reading called "*Your Pet and Worms*". (Oh, nice. Very nice.)

"Turn the cage round the other way, Ellie," he said.

Ellie turned my cage round the other way.

Now I was looking at the Fisher's terrier. (And if there's any animal in the world who ought to have HANDLE WITH CARE written at the top of his case notes, it's the Fisher's terrier).

Okay, so I hissed at him. It was only a little hiss. You practically had to have bionic ears to *hear* it.

And I did growl a bit. But you'd think he'd have a head start on growling. He is a dog, after all. I'm only a cat.

And yes, okay, I spat a bit. But only a bit. Nothing you'd even *notice* unless you were waiting to pick on someone.

Well, how was *I* to know he wasn't feeling very well? Not *everyone* waiting for the vet is ill. *I* wasn't ill, was I? Actually, I've never been ill in my life. I don't even know what it *feels* like. But I reckon, even if I were *dying*, something furry locked in a cage could make an eensy-weensy noise at me

without my ending up whimpering and cowering, and scrabbling to get under the seat, to hide behind the knees of my owner.

More a *chicken* than a Scotch terrier, if you want my opinion.

"Could you please keep that vile cat of yours under control?" Mrs Fisher said nastily.

Ellie stuck up for me.

"He is in a cage!"

"He's still scaring half the animals in here to death. Can't you cover him up, or something?"

Ellie was going to keep arguing, I could tell. But, without even looking up from his worm pamphlet, her father just dropped his raincoat over my cage as if I were some mangy old *parrot* or something.

And everything went black.

No wonder by the time the vet came at me with her nasty long needle, I was in a bit of a mood. I didn't mean to scratch her that badly, though.

Or smash all those little glass bottles.

Or tip the expensive new cat scales off the bench.

Or spill all that cleaning fluid.

It wasn't me who ripped my record card into tiny pieces, though. That was the vet.

When we left, Ellie was in tears again. (Some people are born soft.) She hugged my cage tightly to her chest.

"Oh, Tuffy! Until we find a new vet who'll promise to look after you, you must be so careful not to get run over."

"Fat chance!" her father muttered.

I was just glowering at him through the cage wire, when he spotted Ellie's mother, standing knee-deep in shopping bags outside the supermarket.

"You're very late," she scolded. "Was there a bit of trouble at the vet's?"

Ellie burst into tears. I mean, talk about *wimp*. But her father is made of sterner stuff. He'd just taken the most huge breath, ready to snitch on me,

44

when suddenly he let it out again. Out of the corner of his eye, he'd spotted trouble of another sort.

"Quick!" he whispered. "Next-door is just coming through the check-out."

He picked up half the shopping bags. Ellie's mother picked up the rest. But before we could get away, next-door had come through the glass doors.

So now all four of them were forced to chat.

"Morning," said Ellie's father.

"Morning," said Next-door.

"Nice day," said Ellie's father.

"Lovely," agreed Next-door.

"Nicer than yesterday," said Ellie's mother.

"Oh, yes," Next-door said. "Yesterday was *horrible*."

She probably just meant the

weather, for heaven's sake. But Ellie's
eyes filled with tears. (I don't know
why she was so fond of Thumper. *I'm*
the one who's supposed to be her pet,
not *him*.) And because she couldn't see
where she was going properly any
more, she bumped into her mother,
and half the tins of catfood fell out of
one of the shopping bags, and rolled off
down the street.

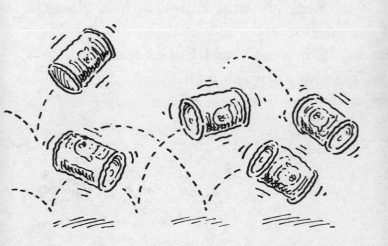

Ellie dumped down my cage, and chased off after them. Then she made the mistake of reading the labels.

"Oh, nooo!" she wailed. "Rabbit chunks!"

(Really, that child is such a *drip*. She'd never make it in our gang. She wouldn't last a *week*.)

"Talking about rabbit," said Next-door. "The most extraordinary thing happened at our house."

"Really?" said Ellie's father, glaring at me.

"Oh, yes?" said Ellie's mother, glaring at me as well.

"Yes," said Next-door. "On
Monday, poor Thumper looked a little
bit poorly, so we brought him inside.
And on Tuesday, he was worse. And
on Wednesday he died. He was
terribly old, and he'd had a happy life,
so we didn't feel too bad about it. In

fact we had a little funeral, and buried
him in a box at the bottom of the
garden."

I'm staring up at the clouds now.

"And on Thursday, he'd gone."

"Gone?"

"Gone?"

"Yes, gone. And all there was left of him was a hole in the ground and an empty box."

"Really?"

"Good heavens!"

Ellie's father was giving me the most suspicious look.

"And then, yesterday," Next-door went on. "Something even more extraordinary happened. Thumper was back again. All fluffed up nicely, and back in his hutch."

"Back in his hutch, you say?"

"Fluffed up nicely? How strange!"

You have to hand it to them, they're good actors. They kept it up all the way home.

"What an amazing story!"

"How on earth could it have happened?"

"Quite astonishing!"

"So strange!"

Till we were safely through the front door. And then, of course, the pair of them turned on me.

"Deceitful creature!"

"Making us think you killed him!"

"Just pretending all along!"

"I *knew* that cat could never have done it. That rabbit was even fatter than he is!"

You'd have thought they all *wanted* me to have murdered old Thumper.

All except Ellie. She was *sweet*.

"Don't you *dare* pick on Tuffy!" she told them. "You leave him alone! I bet he didn't even dig poor Thumper up. I bet it was the Fisher's nasty, vicious terrier who did that. All Tuffy did was bring Thumper back to us so we could make sure he was buried again properly. He's a hero. A kind and thoughtful hero."

She gave me a big soft squeeze.

"Isn't that right, Tuffy?"

I'm saying nothing, am I? I'm a cat.
So I just sat and watched while they
unnailed the cat-flap.

Just when you thought it was safe to go back
in the garden ... Tuffy is back!

The Return of the Killer Cat

Read on for a sneak preview of the
first chapter of this deliciously sharp and
funny follow-up to *The Diary of a Killer Cat*,
out in the shops now!

1: How it began

OKAY, OKAY! SO slap my teensy little furry paws. I messed up.

Big time!

And okay! Tug my tail! It all turned into a bit of a one-cat crime wave.

So what are you going to do? Confiscate my food bowl and tell me I'm a very bad pussy?

But we cats aren't *supposed* to hang about like dogs, doing exactly as we're told, and staring devotedly into your eyes while we wonder if there is some slipper we can fetch you.

We run our own lives, we cats do. I

like running mine. And if there's one
thing I can't stand, it's wasting the
days and nights when the family are
on holiday.

'Oh, Tuffy!' fretted Ellie, giving me
the Big Farewell Squeeze. (I gave her
the cool blink that means: 'Careful,
Ell! Stay on the right side of cuddle

2

here, or you'll get the Big Scratch in return.') 'Oh, Tuffy! We'll be away for a whole week!'

A whole week? Magic words! A whole week of sunning myself in the flower beds without Ellie's mother shrieking, 'Tuffy! Get out of there! You're flattening whole patches!'

A whole week of lolling about on top of the telly without Ellie's father's endless nagging: 'Tuffy! Shift your tail! It's dangling over the goalmouth!'

And, best of all, a whole week of not being scooped up and shoved in next-door's old straw baby basket and stroked and petted by Ellie and her soppy friend Melanie.

'Ooh, you are lucky, Ellie! I wish *I* had a a pet like Tuffy. He's so soft and furry.'

Of course I'm soft and furry. I'm a *cat*.

And I am clever, too. Clever enough to realize it wasn't Mrs Tanner coming to house-and-cat-sit as usual . . .

'. . . no, she suddenly had to rush off to her daughter in Dorset . . . so if you hear of anyone who could do it

. . . only six days . . . well, if you're *sure*, Vicar. Yes, well. So long as you're comfortable with cats . . .'

Who cares if the vicar's comfortable?
I'm the cat.

The Return of the
Killer Cat

'OKAY, OKAY!
So slap my
teensy little
paws. I messed
up – big time.'

Tuffy can't
wait for Ellie
and the family to go away on holiday. He
and the gang plan to ignore the grumpy new
catsitter, and run wild all night.

But could that furry bundle, suddenly flying
through the air, put a stop to all the fun?

The deliciously sharp and funny follow-up to
The Diary of a Killer Cat

THE
SAME OLD STORY
EVERY YEAR

"I have a surprise . . .
This class is
going to do the
Christmas
play!"

Maya longs to
be in Mr Kelly's play!
She can already see herself on the
stage, waving her arms around and
saying her words so loudly everyone
at the back can hear. Wonderful!

But then there's an unexpected
problem . . .

Roll Over Roly

"Jump, you
dozy lump!
Up! Down!
Faster!"

Rupert's puppy,
Roly, is so round and
warm and soft and lovely
that Rupert hasn't the
heart to be stern with him. It
looks as if Roly will *never* learn to behave.
But then he meets a parrot named Gordon...

'Can Anne Fine do no wrong?'
– *Books for Keeps*

'Anne Fine – infectiously funny and
highly readable' – *Independent*

Only a Show

Anna had told herself a
hundred times that it
didn't matter – it was
only a show . . .

Everyone in
Anna's class
must do a
five-minute show,
but she can't think of anything. Why
would anyone listen to her? Anna's
mum and her brother keep telling her
she is special, *very* special. But will
the rest of her class agree?

Jennifer's Diary

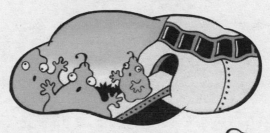

**Nothing much happened today.
After the spaceship landed and all
the blobmen had blobbled down
the ladder into the woods...**

Jennifer has a diary. Iolanthe
doesn't. What Iolanthe has are
ideas. Zillions of ideas for stories
are spilling out of her. But what she
wants is... Jennifer's diary.

'Anne Fine knows how
to make readers laugh'
— *Guardian*

The Worst Child I Ever Had

'It was the worst sight that I have ever seen in all my years of babysitting.'

Why does Mrs Mackle think Susan Solly is the worst child ever? Just what did Susan do that was so terrible? And what did it have to do with snails?

'Anne Fine knows how to make readers laugh' – *Guardian*

'When it comes
to a story,
I just tell 'em
better.'

goggle-eyes

Kitty Killin is not only a good storyteller,
but also the World's Great Expert when
it comes to mothers having new and
unwanted boyfriends. Particularly when
there's a danger they might turn into
new and unwanted stepfathers ...

'*Goggle-Eyes* is a winner: witty, sensitive and
warm-hearted ... a lovely book' – *Guardian*

Winner of the Carnegie Medal and
the *Guardian* Children's Fiction Award

crummy mummy and me

'I don't think my mum's
fit to be a parent,
really I don't.'

How would you feel if
your mother had
royal-blue hair and wore
lavender fishnet tights?
But Minna's whole family
(including her mum's punk
boyfriend, Crusher Maggot) is
a bit unusual. Being the only
sensible one is not easy
for Minna.

'Hilariously readable'
– *Guardian*

Notso Hotso

So, suddenly one morning I'm like, *Scratch-scratch! Scratch-scratch!* and can't stop. It's disgusting.

It's a dog's life for Anthony. Not only is he lacking the respect he deserves from the neighbourhood dogs and cats, but bits of him are dropping off! And just when Anthony thinks things can't get worse, he finds himself on the vet's table. What she has in mind for him is likely to destroy the tiny shred of street cred he has left...

'...a fable about embarrassment that made me laugh aloud' – *Independent*

'A wickedly funny tale' – *Carousel*

**Let it be flour babies.
Let chaos reign.**

When the annual school science fair comes round, Mr Cartright's class don't get to work on the Soap Factory, the Maggot Farm or the Exploding Custard Tins. To their intense disgust they get the Flour Babies – sweet little six-pound bags of flour that must be cared for at all times.

Winner of the Whitbread Children's Book Award and the Carnegie Medal

'Funny and moving, *Flour Babies* is an uplifting, self-raising story' – *Guardian*

flour babies

madame doubtfire

**A vast apparition towered
over her on the doorstep.
'I'm Madame Doubtfire, dear.'**

Lydia, Christopher and Natalie Hilliard are
used to domestic turmoil, and have been torn
between their warring parents ever since the
divorce. That all changes when their mother
takes on a most unusual cleaning lady...

Madame Doubtfire inspired the highly
successful film *Mrs Doubtfire*.

'This author can make you laugh and cry
and is too much of a treasure to be reserved
for children alone' – *Independent*

Runner-up for the *Guardian* Children's
Fiction Award and shortlisted for the
Observer Teenage Fiction Prize

a pack of liars

'You can't just write *a pack of lies*!'

All the penpals Laura and Oliver get are
either so boring they send you to sleep,
or complete basket cases. Tedious
Miranda is the last straw. So Laura
writes back and weaves a fantastic
tissue of lies about herself and her
exotic life. But Laura isn't the only one
making things up...

Read and weep . . .

One stormy night, five stranded
schoolchildren uncover the story of
Richard Clayton Harwick — a boy who
many years ago learned what it was like to have
a truly wicked stepfather. But the children have
stories of their own step-parents to tell — stories
that have warmth and humour, as well as sadness,
and a fair share of happy endings.

'For children who have some similar
experience, this novel will be therapeutic;
for those who haven't it's an absorbing read,
to make them laugh and cry'
— *Sunday Telegraph*

step by wicked step

Read more in Puffin

For complete information about books available from Puffin – and Penguin – and how to
order them, contact us at the appropriate address below. Please note that for copyright
reasons the selection of books varies from country to country.

www.puffin.co.uk

In the United Kingdom: Please write to Dept EP, Penguin Books Ltd,
Bath Road, Harmondsworth, West Drayton, Middlesex UB7 0DA

In the United States: Please write to Penguin Group (USA), Inc. P.O. Box 12289,
Dept B, Newark, New Jersey 07101–5289 or call 1–800–788–6262

In Canada: Please write to Penguin Books Canada Ltd,
10 Alcorn Avenue, Suite 300, Toronto, Ontario M4V 3B2

In Australia: Please write to Penguin Books Australia Ltd,
250 Camberwell Road, Camberwell, Victoria 3124

In New Zealand: Please write to Penguin Books (NZ) Ltd,
Private Bag 102902, North Shore Mail Centre, Auckland 10

In India: Please write to Penguin Books India Pvt Ltd,
11 Panscheel Shopping Centre, Panscheel Park, New Delhi 110 017

In the Netherlands: Please write to Penguin Books Netherlands bv,
Postbus 3507, NL–1001 AH Amsterdam

In Germany: Please write to Penguin Books Deutschland GmbH,
Metzlerstrasse 26, 60594 Frankfurt am Main

In Spain: Please write to Penguin Books S. A., Bravo Murillo 19,
1° B, 28015 Madrid

In Italy: Please write to Penguin Italia s.r.l.,
Via Felice Casati 20, I–20124 Milano

In France: Please write to Penguin France S. A.,
17 rue Lejeune, F–31000 Toulouse

In Japan: Please write to Penguin Books Japan, Ishikiribashi Building,
2–5–4, Suido, Bunkyo-ku, Tokyo 112

In South Africa: Please write to Longman Penguin Southern Africa (Pty) Ltd,
Private Bag X08, Bertsham 2013